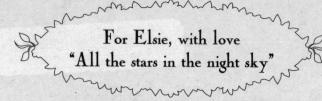

For Elsie, with love
"All the stars in the night sky"

Special thanks to Valerie Wilding

ISBN 978-0-545-90745-3

Text copyright © 2015 by Working Partners Limited
Illustrations © 2015 by Working Partners Limited

Series author: Daisy Meadows

All rights reserved. Published by Scholastic Inc., *Publishers since 1920*, by arrangement with Working Partners Limited. Series created by Working Partners Limited, London.

10 9 8 7 6 5 4 3   17 18 19 20

Printed in the U.S.A.   40
First printing 2016

Ruby Fuzzybrush's Star Dance

Daisy Meadows

Scholastic Inc.

Shining House

Sunshine Meadow

Blossom Briar

Goldie's Grotto

Toadstool Café

Toadstool Glade

Mrs. Taptree's Library

Friendship Tree

Maze

Silver Spring

Buttercup Grove

Lighthouse

Can you keep a secret? I thought you could!

Then I'll tell you about an enchanted wood.

It lies through the door in the old oak tree.

Let's go there now—just follow me!

We'll find adventure that never ends,

And meet the Magic Animal Friends!

Love,
Goldie the Cat

Contents

CHAPTER ONE

Sunset in the Forest

As it got dark, Lily Hart and her best friend, Jess Forester, grinned at each other excitedly. They'd been waiting all day for the sun to go down, so that some very special animals would wake up! As they left the barn, the last of the sunshine lit up the sign on the door: HELPING PAW

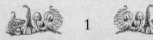

WILDLIFE HOSPITAL. Lily's parents had set up the hospital to take care of all kinds of animals, and Lily and Jess helped out there whenever they could.

"I'm so excited," Jess said, twirling one of her blond curls around her finger. "I've never fed a fox cub before."

"Me neither!" said Lily. "Wait until you see them, they're adorable!"

"You forgot these!" Mrs. Hart came out of the hospital and handed them each a feeding bottle full of milk and a flashlight. "Here you go," she said. "Have fun!"

Lily took Jess over to one of the special

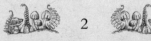

runs her dad had made to keep the animal patients safe. It had a lid made of wire netting on a wooden frame. As Lily lifted it, two fluffy little faces with pointed noses and amber eyes peeped sleepily out from a wooden shelter.

"They're so cute!" exclaimed Jess.

"A lady from the village found them all alone yesterday afternoon," Lily said, shaking her head so that her short dark hair swung around her face. "Dad said foxes are nocturnal, so they're supposed to sleep during the day and be awake at night."

The girls knelt down next to the run. The cubs tottered over on wobbly legs, with their long fluffy tails trailing in the grass. Soon they were guzzling the warm milk greedily.

When the bottles were empty, Jess
and Lily replaced the wire cover. The
sun was going down, but the cubs were
wide awake. Lily and Jess turned on
their flashlights and stayed to watch
as the cute little fox
cubs played with
each other.

As she looked at them, Lily caught sight of something else glowing: two shining eyes! Something was crouched underneath a nearby bush.

"Look, Jess," she whispered. "Maybe it's another fox cub."

As she spoke, the creature appeared.

"Even better—it's Goldie!" Lily gasped in delight.

A beautiful golden cat bounded over and curled around their legs.

 6

The girls shared a wonderful secret
with the little cat—she lived in Friendship
Forest, a hidden world where all the
animals could talk! Now both girls were
smiling with excitement.

"If Goldie's here, that means we're
going back to Friendship Forest!" cried
Jess happily.

"A nighttime adventure with our
animal friends!" Lily grinned in delight.

The cat immediately turned toward
Brightley Stream, which ran across
the bottom of the Harts' yard. Using the
beams from their flashlights, Jess and Lily

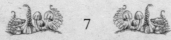

followed Goldie over the stepping-stones and into Brightley Meadow.

Lily shone her flashlight on a lifeless old oak tree in the middle of the meadow—the Friendship Tree. She glanced at Jess excitedly, knowing what would happen as they drew near.

Sure enough, the old tree burst into life. As leaves sprouted from every twig, a nightingale sang sweetly from the topmost branch

and pale moths
danced around the
yellow flower buds that
dotted the grass below. Lily and
Jess gasped. They'd never seen the
Friendship Tree in the dark before.
"It looks so different from how
it is in the day," said Lily, "but
just as beautiful!"
The girls read aloud the words
carved into the tree's bark.
"Friendship Forest!" they
said together.

They felt a thrill as a small door with a leaf-shaped handle appeared in the trunk. When Jess opened it, shimmering golden light poured out.

Goldie darted inside.

"I can't wait to see everyone again!" exclaimed Lily.

Tucking their flashlights into their pockets, the girls stooped to follow Goldie.

Instantly, they tingled all over, and knew that they were shrinking, just a little.

As the golden light faded, Jess and Lily found themselves once more in beautiful, flower-scented Friendship Forest. The

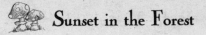

sun was setting here, too, casting long shadows, and the flowers were closing up for the evening.

Lily looked back. "The Friendship Tree's leaves aren't golden anymore," she said in surprise. "They're turning silver!"

"That's because it's nearly nighttime," said a soft voice.

The girls spun around. "Goldie!" they cried, rushing to hug her.

The green-eyed cat was standing
upright, wearing her golden scarf. As the
girls were smaller, Goldie almost reached
up to their shoulders, and now that they
were in Friendship Forest, she could talk!

"It's so nice to see you," Jess told their
friend. Then she noticed that Goldie's
tail was twitching anxiously. "What is it,
Goldie? Are Grizelda's dragons causing
trouble again?"

Grizelda was an evil witch who wanted
to make the animals leave Friendship
Forest so she could have it all for herself.
The girls had managed to stop her

 12

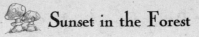

wicked plans so far, but now she had dragons helping her!

Goldie sighed. "I think one of the dragons must be up to something. The Fuzzybrush fox family say they've seen strange things in the sky."

The girls stared at Goldie in dismay.

"It sounds like Grizelda has an awful new plan," said Lily.

"Whatever it is," said Jess fiercely, "we'll stop her. We won't let her or her dragons hurt Friendship Forest, Goldie—we promise!"

CHAPTER TWO

The Magical Moonstone

The setting sun streaked the sky above
Friendship Forest with pinks and reds.
As they walked through the forest,
Lily waved to some birds who were
snuggling down for the night in their nest
in a hollow tree.

 15

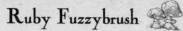

"Good night!"
chirruped the
smallest bird,
yawning sleepily.

"Sleep well!"
Jess called to the cute little birds.

"Everyone's going to bed!" Lily said.

"Not everyone!" Goldie said with
a smile. "There are lots of nocturnal
animals in Friendship Forest. Like the
Fuzzybrush fox family."

"We'd better talk to them about the
strange things they saw," Jess said.

"Where do they live?" Lily asked.

The cat smiled. "In a very unusual home," she said. "You'll see!"

After a while, a tall, narrow building came into view. Soft light glowed from the circular window at the top.

"It's a lighthouse!" cried Jess. "An orange-and-white-striped lighthouse!"

"The Fuzzybrushes keep the lighthouse night-light on when it's dark," Goldie explained. "With that and the stars, all the nighttime animals can see their way around the forest."

"Wow," breathed Lily. "Do you think the Fuzzybrushes would let us see inside?"

 17

Before Goldie could reply, a door on the side of the lighthouse opened and the Fuzzybrush family ran out to meet them. Two larger foxes and two cubs bounded around the girls in a whirl of pointed noses, orange fur, and fluffy tails.

"Welcome to our home," said Mrs. Fuzzybrush proudly.

The adorable fox cubs bounded excitedly around the girls. The girl cub had a pretty bow around her neck, and the boy had a baseball cap on.

"Do you remember us?" the girl fox asked eagerly.

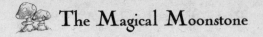

"Of course we do, Ruby," said Lily. "And you too, Rusty!" She gave them each a big hug.

The brave cubs had helped Goldie and the girls defeat Grizelda in their adventure with little Bella Tabbypaw the kitten.

"Could you tell us about the thing you saw in the sky?" Goldie asked Mr. and Mrs. Fuzzybrush.

"It was a black shadow, as big as me," said Mr. Fuzzybrush in a gruff voice, "and it glided over the forest."

"It was spooky!" said Ruby. Rusty nodded in agreement.

The girls and Goldie exchanged glances. "This must be something to do with Grizelda," Lily whispered.

Mrs. Fuzzybrush glanced up at the darkening sky. "The sun's almost set, children," she called, "so it's—"

"Star dance time!" cried Ruby.

Jess was puzzled. "What's a star dance?" she asked.

"Come with us," said Mr. Fuzzybrush kindly, "and we'll show you!"

Everyone followed him inside the lighthouse. On the ground floor were a comfortable living room and three cozy bedrooms.

"That one's mine!" said Ruby proudly, as they passed a pretty, round room decorated in red and pink.

"It's the color of rubies!" said Lily.

Rusty rushed them past his bedroom.

"Mine's a little messy," he said.
The girls peeked inside and
smiled as they saw a building
set and little toy foxes scattered
messily all over the bedroom floor.
They went up a spiral staircase
right to the very top of the
lighthouse. In the middle of
the floor was a wooden
star-shaped table.

Sitting on top
of it was a
smooth,
white stone

the size of a watermelon. It glowed with a
soft, pretty light.

"That's so beautiful," breathed Lily.
"What is it?"

"It's the magical moonstone,"
Mr. Fuzzybrush explained. "We need
it for our star dance. Every evening we
dance around it, to wake the stars. Then
at dawn, we dance again to put them
back to sleep."

"The star dance is a special dance that
only foxes know," said Goldie. "It takes a
really long time to learn."

"It's getting dark now," said

Mrs. Fuzzybrush, "which means it's time for our star dance! Come on, children, let's go to the clearing!"

Mrs. Fuzzybrush carefully picked up the moonstone and raced down the spiral staircase.

Lily and Jess followed the foxes as they hurried into a clearing next to the lighthouse. Mrs. Fuzzybrush put the magical moonstone down in the center and gave it a brush with her tail.

Ruby tugged at Lily's skirt. "Rusty and I know all the steps now!"

The Fuzzybrushes took up their

positions around the magical moonstone and began to dance.

Goldie, Jess, and Lily watched in delight. The foxes stepped, dipped, glided, and turned around the moonstone, weaving complicated patterns. Each time they swept past each other and their bushy tails touched, the glow from the moonstone grew brighter.

Lily glanced up at the night sky. "Look, Jess!" she whispered. "The stars are coming out."

Jess gazed at the sky. "It's so beautiful!" she cried. "Oh! The brighter the

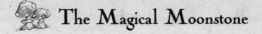

moonstone becomes, the more stars appear."

The girls stared in delight as hundreds—no, thousands—of stars winked and blinked in the darkness. Soon it was almost as bright as daytime, as the forest lit up with sparkling silver starlight.

Suddenly, Rusty cried out, "Look, Mom, Dad! Up there in the sky!"

Everyone stopped dancing and turned to stare.

A dark shadow, just as Mr. Fuzzybrush had described, was flying through the night sky.

Jess and Lily watched as it came closer.

"That's not a shadow," Lily said shakily.

"You're right," cried Jess. "It's one of Grizelda's dragons!"

CHAPTER THREE

Smudge the Dragon

The black dragon zoomed closer.

"He's heading right toward the lighthouse!" cried Jess.

As he flew, the dragon's long, scaly tail tangled around his back legs. He beat his black wings harder as he tried to swerve aside, but it was too late.

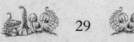

Crash! He bashed into the lighthouse roof and skidded on the tiles.

Ruby scooped up the moonstone and the foxes ran toward their home, followed by Goldie and the girls. As they got to the lighthouse, everyone gasped.

Long curved claws scrabbled at the roof. A cloud of soot puffed over the lighthouse, blocking out the night-light that shone through the windows. Immediately, the forest went darker. The dragon scrambled over the roof and Ruby ducked as a tile crashed down.

The dragon peered down at the foxes.

Then he took off from the roof and
circled around, lower and lower, until
his tail caught around his wing and he
*bump-bump-bump*ed to the ground,
sending up another puff of soot.

"He's so clumsy!" said Lily.

"And dirty!" said Goldie. She pointed to

the lighthouse, which was smeared with black soot. "What a mess! Grizelda called him Smudge, remember? No wonder!"

Smudge spotted something and grinned. Then he shook his wing free from his tail and swooped down toward Ruby Fuzzybrush.

"*Raargh!*" he roared, as he grabbed the magical moonstone out of her paws.

Jess heard Ruby start to

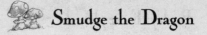

cry and knelt down to stroke the cub's
soft, furry head.

"No more night-light and no more
stars." Smudge laughed. "The night
should be the darkest dark."

Mr. Fuzzybrush folded his paws crossly.
"Give that back," he said to Smudge.
"We need the moonstone to make
starlight so all the nighttime animals can
find their way."

Smudge stumbled over his tail
as he landed and waddled over to
Mr. Fuzzybrush. "Grizelda wants the
forest to be dark, and so do I," he said.

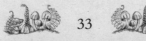

"So there!" He took a deep breath and huffed a great sooty cloud all over the foxes.

Lily and Jess expected them to start coughing. But they didn't. When the sooty cloud cleared, Mr. and Mrs. Fuzzybrush and Rusty had completely vanished!

"Hee hee!" Smudge giggled. He flapped his wings and took off. There was a sound of snapping branches as he crashed through the trees on his way back up into the night sky.

Beside Jess, Ruby stared in horror at the place where her family had been. "Mom!

 34

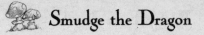

Dad! Rusty! They disappeared!" she

cried. "Where are they?"

"I don't know," said Jess, looking around

desperately.

"Oh, no!" cried Lily. "The stars are

disappearing, too!"

"The moonstone!" Ruby wailed. "The

stars are fading because Smudge has

the moonstone and we didn't finish the

dance!" The little fox cub sniffled

miserably. Then her eyes widened.

"What's that?"

Lily and Jess looked, and groaned.

A familiar yellow-green orb was flying

toward them. With a *cra-ack!* it exploded
in a huge shower of nasty-smelling,
yellow-green sparks and Grizelda
appeared. Her long green hair snaked
around her thin, bony face.

"Grizelda!" said Jess. "What did
Smudge do to the
Fuzzybrushes? Tell
him to bring them
back right now!"

The witch
threw back her
cloak, revealing
her shiny purple

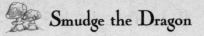

tunic and pants, and her pointy-toed
boots.

"Ha haaa!" she cackled. "No more
starlight! The nighttime animals will get
lost and fall down holes and bump into
things, because they won't be able to see.
Then they'll have to leave the forest! Ha
ha haaa!"

The girls glared at her. Ruby hid
behind Jess's legs.

"That's not all," Grizelda said gleefully.
"No more starlight means no more
Friendship Tree."

"What?" gasped Lily.

"Without starlight, the silver leaves
will fall from the Friendship Tree," Goldie
explained. "And without its leaves, it will
lose its magic."

The girls were horrified.

"But doesn't that mean . . ." Jess began.

Goldie nodded sadly. "You wouldn't be
able to come back to Friendship Forest
ever again."

CHAPTER FOUR

Shadow Spell

Grizelda gave a wicked laugh. "You interfering girls had better go home before the last leaf on the Friendship Tree falls," she said scornfully, "or you'll be stuck here forever!"

Lily and Jess glanced at each other. The thought of never seeing their animal

friends again was awful, but so was never

being able to go home.

"Oh, Goldie," said Lily with a sob.

"We have to go! We couldn't leave our

families."

"Yes, go!" sneered Grizelda. "Go away!

No more meddling in my plans. Ha haaa!"

She snapped her fingers and

disappeared in a burst of smelly yellow

sparks.

"I can't imagine never coming to

Friendship Forest again," Lily said. Tears

filled her eyes. "We'd miss you so much!"

Jess put an arm around Lily. She felt like

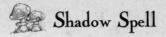

crying, too. "How long do you think we have before the Friendship Tree loses its magic?" she asked.

Goldie looked up at the fading stars. "The last leaf will fall when the last star fades from the sky," she said grimly.

Jess and Lily looked up.

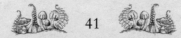

"We have to try to stop Grizelda's plan," said Jess determinedly. "If only we could get the Fuzzybrushes and the moonstone back . . . they could dance and bring out the stars again. Then we can stay here."

"Where should we start looking?" Lily asked Goldie.

But the cat was staring at the lighthouse. Her green eyes had narrowed and her tail twitched thoughtfully.

"What is it, Goldie?" asked Lily. "Have you seen something?"

Goldie pointed at the lighthouse wall.

"Look at those funny shadows," she said. "I can't see what's casting them."

Ruby gave a squeal. "One of them's waving!" she cried.

They peered closer.

"Each shadow has two pointy ears," said Lily.

"And a bushy tail," Jess added. "Oh my goodness, they're—"

"Foxes!" cried Goldie. "Smudge turned the Fuzzybrushes into shadows!"

Ruby ran over to the lighthouse and tried to hug one of the shadow foxes, but she couldn't.

Lily put her arm around Ruby and kissed the top of her head. "Don't worry," she said. "We'll make Smudge reverse his magic and give us the moonstone. You'll get your family back."

Ruby wiped her eyes with her tail. "And then we'll bring out the stars again," she said firmly.

Jess tickled the cub's fluffy ears. "You're a very brave little fox," she said.

Goldie had been thinking. "I wonder," she said, "if any of the nighttime animals are in Toadstool Glade. Maybe someone saw where Smudge went."

"We have to hurry," Lily said. As she stared up at the sky, one star blinked out, then another.

The forest was so much quieter than when all the animals were awake. A few of the little cottages they passed still had

lights on in the windows, but most of
them were dark.

"Look!" Lily pointed to the Toadstool
Café. A light was shining from the
window. Lily, Jess, Goldie, and Ruby
rushed over to peek inside. Lucy
Longwhiskers the rabbit and her dad
waved to
them from the
window, then
came out to
see them.
Lucy was
wearing

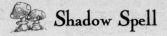

spotty pink pajamas and fluffy rabbit slippers.

"Lucy couldn't sleep, so I was just making her some hot chocolate," Mr. Longwhiskers explained. "Would you like some, too?"

"I'm afraid we don't have time," said Goldie. She quickly explained what had happened.

The rabbits were shocked.

"Poor you," Lucy said, hugging Ruby. "You must be so worried."

"I am," said the fox cub. "We have to find Smudge. Have you seen him?"

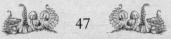

The rabbits sadly shook their heads. But then Mr. Longwhiskers hopped up and down excitedly. "You could go to the Midnight Market," he suggested.

"What's the Midnight Market?" asked Jess curiously.

"I know!" Ruby scampered off. "I'll tell you on the way!"

"Thank you!" the girls and Goldie called to the Longwhiskers as they raced after Ruby.

"The Midnight Market is where all the nighttime animals buy things," Goldie

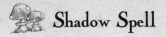

explained. "I don't know why we didn't think of it before!"

"Rusty and I always buy star cookies at the market," said Ruby as they passed the Friendship Tree. "We could get some for him. Star cookies are his favorite treat," she added sadly.

Goldie hugged her. "That's a great idea," she said.

As they passed the Friendship Tree, Lily caught

sight of a silver pile on the ground.
"What's that?" she wondered out loud.

Goldie gave a gasp. "Leaves!"

Lily and Jess glanced at each other
in dismay. The Friendship Tree's lower
branches were already drooping, and the
silver leaves were fading to a pale, ghostly
gray. As they watched, another one
fluttered down to the ground.

Lily shuddered. "Come on," she said
bravely. "We have to hurry! If we don't
find that dragon soon, the Friendship Tree
will lose its magic forever!"

CHAPTER FIVE

The Midnight Market

Ruby bounded through the dark forest
and stopped at a tall oak tree. "We're
here!" the fox cub said happily. "The
Midnight Market!"

"But where is it?" Lily asked, looking
around in amazement. She could hear lots
of voices, but she couldn't see anyone!

"Look up!" Ruby pointed her paw. Way above them, high in the trees, was a huge circular platform.

Jess peered around the tree trunks. It was getting darker and darker as one by one the stars faded. Suddenly she remembered her flashlight. She pulled it out of her pocket and switched it on. "How do we get up there?" she asked, swinging her flashlight around. "I can't see a staircase or a ladder."

Ruby grinned. "I'll show you!" She led them to a wooden platform on the ground beneath the middle tree. It had a fence

 52

around the edge with
a gate. A thick loop of
vine hung beside it.
"It's an elevator!" said Jess.
Ruby opened the gate
and they all got onto the
elevator. Then Ruby darted
over to the vine,
tugged it, and up they
went! Up and up, until
the elevator stopped at a
wide wooden walkway
that stretched across the
treetops.

The Midnight Market!

In the middle of the platform there were tables laden with fruit tarts, strawberry toffees, hats, mossy headbands, and necklaces made of nuts and seeds. The market was decorated with vines covered in berries that hung on the edges of the tables and around tree branches.

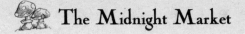

But instead of enjoying themselves, the animals at the market were huddled together, talking in worried voices.

"We're too frightened to fly high," trilled a nightingale, "ever since we heard that there's a shadow dragon nearby."

"Everybody must leap a cookout," said a familiar voice. "I mean, keep a lookout." It was their friend Mr. Cleverfeather the owl, getting his words muddled as usual!

The girls hurried over to him. All the other animals clustered around.

"Hello, Goldie. Hello, Jess and Lily," said Mr. Silverback the badger. "And who's that? Oh, it's little Ruby Fuzzybrush!"

Mr. Cleverfeather introduced the girls to the animals they hadn't met before. The nightingale, who was called Melody Sweetsong, trilled a musical greeting. A little pair of bats called Luna and

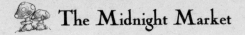

Dusky Longears fluttered around them
with their soft, velvety wings, squeaking,
"Helloelloello!"

Mr. Cleverfeather
waved a wing at
a family of brown
owls. "These are
my cousins, the
Wisefeathers."

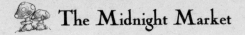

"Hoo hoo," they
said. "We've heard about yoohoo!"

"And this," Mr. Cleverfeather said, "is
Dora Tinytail."

At first, Jess and Lily couldn't see Dora,

but they lowered their flashlights and, in the yellow glow, saw the most adorable little golden dormouse.

When Jess put her hand down, Dora climbed onto it and curled up, with her fluffy tail wrapped around her. She

yawned and immediately fell asleep.

"She's so cute!" said Lily.

"She should try to stay awake," said Mr. Silverback, "in case that dragon appears."

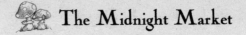

"And what has happened to the light-night and the tars—I mean, the night-light and the stars?" Mr. Cleverfeather asked.

Goldie explained about the poor Fuzzybrushes and the star dance, and how they badly needed to make Smudge reverse his spell. "Have any of you seen him?" she asked.

Everyone shook their heads. "The problem is," said Mr. Silverback, "that even us nighttime animals would have trouble spotting Smudge when it's this dark."

"I'm not surprised," said Jess, glancing up at the sky. There were only a few stars

left. "I can barely see a thing now, even with a flashlight. How can we search the whole forest?"

All the animals looked at each other anxiously.

"What about fireflies?" Jess exclaimed. "They helped us before."

"They live too far away," Goldie said.

"I think I've got just the thing," Mr. Cleverfeather told them. "Some lightbites I was making for a party."

"Lightbites?" Jess said in confusion.

"I mean bright lights," Mr. Cleverfeather said, shaking his head.

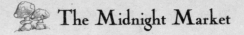

"Those sound perfect!" Lily gasped.

"But they're all the way over at my workshop." Mr. Cleverfeather sighed.

"Yoohoo start looking, and we'll fly and get them," Mrs. Wisefeather volunteered. "Then we'll come and find yoohoo!" The brown owls flapped their wings and sped off.

"They won't be back soon enough." Goldie looked worried as another star disappeared.

"But we have to find Smudge!" Ruby cried, leaning against a tree trunk and cuddling her tail sadly.

As she looked at the tiny fox, Jess gave a cry. "Ruby, look at your tail!"

The fox cub shook her tail. Black dust came off.

Lily put her hand against the tree trunk. It was covered in soot!

"Look!" Lily cried. "I know how to find Smudge! All we have to do is follow the trail of soot!"

"There's more over hereherehere!" called Luna Longears.

Mr. Cleverfeather pointed a wing.

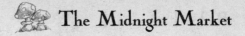

"Wish they, everyone—I mean, this way! Keep looking for the soot!"

Lily and Jess shone their flashlights ahead. The narrow beams didn't show much, but with all the nighttime animals working together, they were finding the trail.

Jess could hear Ruby's footsteps as the little cub scampered along beside them.

"We don't want anyone to let gost— I mean, get lost," said Mr. Cleverfeather. "Goldie, hold my wing tip. Jess, you hold her paw, and Lily can hold Jess's arm. Ruby, you hold on to Lily."

All the nighttime animals held on to one another as they walked carefully through the forest.

Occasionally one of the animals called out as they spotted some soot on a tree

branch or bush where Smudge had bumped his way along.

It got darker and darker as the stars went out one by one. The animals

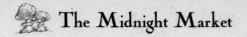

huddled together, trying to search by the light of the girls' flashlights.

Finally they spotted a faint glow ahead. "Is it the Wisefeathers with the lights?" Goldie asked.

"No! That's the moonstone!" Ruby cried, racing forward.

"Quick!" cried Lily.

The girls rushed after her, into the

shadowy darkness of the forest. Jess's
foot caught a fallen branch, and she
tripped.

"Ow!" she cried.

"Are you OK?" asked Lily, stopping to
help her up.

"I'm fine," Jess said.

Suddenly there was a chuckle in the
tree next to them. The girls swung around,
shining their flashlights toward the noise.
There, wrapped around the trunk, was
Smudge the dragon!

Smudge gave another laugh. "Hee,
hee! Nice darkness makes everyone else

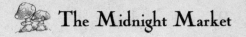

fall over, too!" Then he scrambled inside a hollow in a tree trunk, taking the moonstone with him.

Lily turned to Jess in excitement. "So that's why Smudge likes the dark so much," she said. "In the dark, he's not the only one who's clumsy!"

"If we can show him how to stop tripping over all the time, maybe he'll lift the spell on the Fuzzybrushes," Jess said.

"Great idea!" said Lily. "The stars
will come back and the Friendship
Tree will be safe. We just need to figure
out how to teach a dragon not to be
clumsy . . ."

CHAPTER SIX

Ruby's Dance

After Lily and Jess had told the others their idea, Goldie's whiskers drooped. "It's a great plan, girls," she said, "but how will we stop Smudge tripping over? I can't think of anything."

Ruby jumped up and down excitedly. "But I can!" she cried.

"What's your plan, Ruby?" asked Lily.

Ruby swished her tail. "Remember the star dance we showed you?"

The girls and Goldie nodded.

"When Rusty and I first started learning it, our tails got in the way," Ruby said. "But once we'd learned some dance moves, we stopped tripping over them. Dancing's really good for learning how to keep your balance, you see," she added.

Jess grinned—she'd guessed what Ruby

was thinking. "So if you teach Smudge some dance moves, he'll be less clumsy!"

"And then he won't want to be in the dark anymore, since he won't be tripping all the time," Goldie finished. She reached over and hugged the little cub. "That's brilliant, Ruby!"

"Smudge!" Lily called up at the tree where the dragon was hiding.

Smudge's voice echoed from inside the tree. "Go away!" he grumbled.

"Ruby's going to teach us how to dance," Jess called back. "Why don't you come and join us?"

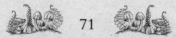

"No!" Smudge. "I'm staying in here."

Ruby looked disappointed, and Lily felt a nervous swirling in her tummy. They had to make Smudge reverse his spell, or the Friendship Tree would lose its magic and the Fuzzybrushes would be shadows forever!

Just then there was a flapping sound and the Wisefeather owls appeared, carrying a long string of beautiful lights in their beaks. The owls perched on the nearby trees and Lily and Jess blinked up at them happily. The golden bright lights twinkled above them like tiny chandeliers.

"Come on, let's make Smudge change his mind!" Jess said determinedly. "Everyone, make some music!"

The nighttime animals gathered in a circle, lit by the golden lights. Melody Sweetsong the nightingale started to sing. Mr. Silverback clapped his paws while the Longears bat family whistled.

Ruby's pointy ears pricked up happily. She held on to her tail with one paw and skipped in a circle. Goldie held her tail and followed after her, while the girls pretended to hold tails, too, and skipped along after them.

"Now hop like this!" Ruby called. She jumped from right to left, waving her tail in the opposite direction. Goldie and the girls copied her, the girls waving a hand instead of a tail. They were all grinning.

"This is so much fun!" cried Jess.

Lily giggled as Ruby started shuffling backward, wiggling her paws in front of her. As she copied the fox cub, she saw Smudge peeking out of the hollow in his tree. He was bobbing his head in time to the music.

"Let's keep going," Lily whispered. "I think it's working!"

Ruby led them in a waltz around Smudge's tree. Every few beats, she paused to kick out a paw and shimmy her tail.

Jess was last in line, and a movement from behind caught her eye.

It was Smudge! He was skipping after them, flapping his wings and dancing!

"Hee!" laughed Smudge, clapping his scaly paws. "Look at me!"

"Hooray!" cried Lily.

They all gathered around the dancing dragon. Ruby took his paw in hers. "Hold your tail in your other paw, like this," she said, showing him, "then hop from foot to foot!"

"Whee!" said Smudge, doing as Ruby said. He finished the move with a flap of his wings and a wiggle of his head.

Goldie clapped. "That's great, Smudge! You're a really good dancer!"

Just then Smudge tripped over his tail. Jess held her breath. If Smudge didn't manage to dance, he might not help the Fuzzybrushes!

But to their relief the dragon wobbled, then turned it into a twirling dance move!

"Good job, Smudge!" Ruby cried.

Jess pointed up at the glittering lights. "We couldn't dance without Mr. Cleverfeather's bright lights, though," she said. "We wouldn't be able to see what we're doing. Smudge, will you lift the spell you put on the Fuzzybrushes? Then you can dance under the stars every night."

Smudge nodded his scaly head. "I want everyone to see me now," he said. "Yes, I'll take away the spell!"

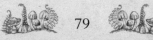

Ruby gave a cry of delight. "I'll get my family back!" she cried.

"And the Friendship Tree will be safe," said Jess, smiling. "Lily and I can keep coming to the forest!"

CHAPTER SEVEN

Starlight

The Wisefeathers flapped through the
forest, holding the bright lights to guide
the way. Smudge flew along beside them,
carrying the magical moonstone. When
his tail got in the way of his legs, he
turned his stumble into a dance move,
hopping and waving his paws.

 81

"Go, Smudge!" cheered Jess.

But a terrible surprise awaited the group as they passed the Friendship Tree.

"There are hardly any leaves left!" Jess gasped. "We're running out of time!"

They raced to the lighthouse, where three fox shadows stood waiting.

"Don't worry, Mom, we're going to take the spell off you," Ruby said.

The two big shadows reached out to the little cub, but stopped when Smudge skipped toward them.

"It's okay," Lily told them. "Smudge is going to free you."

 82

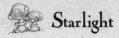

With a final hop, Smudge huffed a dark sooty cloud over the three shadows. It swirled around them, and then, with a puff, it was gone, and there stood Mr. and Mrs. Fuzzybrush and Rusty!

The whole fox family hugged one

another, rolling over and over in a jumble of legs and fluffy tails.

Finally, they got to their feet. Their ears pricked up as Goldie told them about their adventure.

"Thank you for saving us," said Mrs. Fuzzybrush, "and for looking after Ruby."

"She's a very good dance teacher," said Jess. "We couldn't have done it without her!"

Ruby hugged the girls and Goldie. "It was a wonderful adventure," she said, "but I was a little scared."

 84

Mr. Fuzzybrush kissed her nose. "Scared? You?" he said. "No other fox cub has ever been brave enough to teach a dragon how to dance!"

"Speaking of dancing, can you
do your star dance, please?" Jess said,
looking up at the sky. There was just one
little star left.

"Hurry," begged Lily, thinking of the
leaves on the Friendship Tree.

Everyone ran into the clearing. Smudge
put the moonstone in the middle and as

the girls and Goldie watched, the foxes
began their stepping, gliding, twirling
dance. Smudge sat nearby, swishing his
tail in time. As the tips of the foxes' bushy
tails touched, the moonstone began to glow.

"There!" said Jess, pointing up at the
inky sky. A star was twinkling. More and
more appeared, and soon the sky was

dusted with

sparkling starlight.

"Perfect for dancing under!" said Smudge, clapping his paws as he gazed up at the twinkling stars.

As the moonstone shone brighter than ever before, the Fuzzybrushes finished and took a bow. The star dance was complete.

"That looked so magical!" said Jess.

"It *was* magical!" said Lily. "Now the Friendship Tree will be safe."

Ruby was whispering to her parents. They nodded, and she went to stand close to where the black

shadow dragon was perched.

"Smudge, would you like to learn some

more dance moves?" she asked.

"Oh, yes!" Smudge cried.

"Then my mom and dad say that you

can come and stay at the lighthouse with

us," Ruby said, "as long as you promise

not to make everything too sooty."

Smudge flew in a big loop-the-loop, got tangled in his tail, turned it into a hop through the air, and landed in front of the Fuzzybrushes. "Thank you!" he said happily. "I'll be good, I promise!"

Ruby, Rusty, and Smudge held paws and twirled around the moonstone.

Lily and Jess grinned at each other, then ran to join in, followed by the other nighttime animals. They all danced happily under the twinkling stars.

Finally it was time for the girls to go home. They hugged Ruby and her family good-bye, and gave Smudge a hug, too.

As they walked happily back through the forest, Jess turned to Lily and Goldie. "Have you noticed that Grizelda's dragons don't seem to like helping her very much?" she said.

Goldie nodded. "Maybe Grizelda forced them to be her helpers."

"I feel sorry for them," said Lily.

Jess agreed.

"Maybe we should find a way to send them back to wherever they came from," she suggested.

"Do you think we could?" asked Lily. "Oh! Look at the Friendship Tree."

New silver leaves were already appearing on the branches, sparkling in the starlight.

"I'm so glad the tree is safe," said Lily. "Imagine never being able to visit Friendship Forest again!"

Goldie touched a paw to the trunk, and a door appeared. "I'm so happy you girls can still come here," said Goldie.

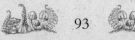

"I don't know what we'd do without you! Grizelda still has one more dragon, and she's bound to cause more trouble soon!"

Lily hugged her. "Whatever she does next, we'll stop her."

"I know you will," said Goldie.

The girls stepped through the door, into the golden light. The tingle began, and they knew they were growing back to their normal size.

As the glow faded, Jess and Lily found themselves back in Brightley Meadow. By the light of their flashlights, they

crossed the stream back to the wildlife hospital.

Jess yawned as they walked up the yard. "I know no time passes while we're in Friendship Forest," she said, "but after that adventure I'm sleepy!"

"Let's check the fox cubs," said Lily, shining her flashlight into the run. Four amber eyes stared back at her, then the cubs carried on chasing each other around and around.

"They look like they're dancing!" said Jess with a laugh.

 95

"Just like the Fuzzybrushes!" Lily looked at her best friend and grinned.

The girls linked arms as they walked home. What magic would they see on their next adventure in Friendship Forest? They couldn't wait to find out!

The End

 96

Grizelda's dragons are causing more trouble in Friendship Forest! Find out if Jess, Lily, Goldie, and little Rosie Gigglepip stop Breezy's terrible storm in their next adventure,

Rosie Gigglepip's Lucky Escape

Turn the page for a sneak peek ...

Friendship Forest was usually filled with warmth and sunshine, but today it looked completely different. The tree branches thrashed around wildly in a fierce wind and leaves and petals swirled through the air. Rain poured down, splashing in puddles everywhere.

"What's happening?" Lily cried, her dark hair whipping around her face.

"It's a storm!" cried Goldie, over the howling wind. "I've never seen one as bad as this!"

Now that they were in the forest, Goldie could talk to them at last. She stood upright beside the girls, almost up to their shoulders, one paw holding her glittery scarf so it couldn't be snatched away by the wind.

As they huddled against the tree trunk, Jess turned to their friend. "Goldie," she cried in alarm, "what's wrong with Friendship Forest?"

Read

Rosie Gigglepip's Lucky Escape

to find out what happens next!

Puzzle Fun!

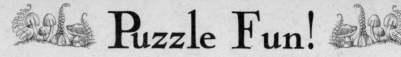

Can you match Ruby Fuzzybrush to the
correct shadow? Do you know who
the other shadows belong to?

A)

B)

C)

ANSWERS

Lily and Jess's Animal Facts

Lily and Jess love lots of different animals—both in Friendship Forest and in the real world.

Here are their top facts about . . .

FOXES

like Ruby Fuzzybrush.

- A fox's tail is called a "brush."

- A female fox is called a "vixen."

- Foxes will eat almost anything, from berries and worms to sausages and jelly sandwiches!

- Foxes have very good hearing and are very fast. Some can run at 30 miles per hour!

- Foxes can jump very high and have been known to climb fences and trees.

- They also have whiskers on their legs as well as their faces. These extra whiskers help them find their way in the dark.

RAINBOW magic™

Which Magical Fairies Have You Met?

- ☐ The Rainbow Fairies
- ☐ The Weather Fairies
- ☐ The Jewel Fairies
- ☐ The Pet Fairies
- ☐ The Dance Fairies
- ☐ The Music Fairies
- ☐ The Sports Fairies
- ☐ The Party Fairies
- ☐ The Ocean Fairies
- ☐ The Night Fairies
- ☐ The Magical Animal Fairies
- ☐ The Princess Fairies
- ☐ The Superstar Fairies
- ☐ The Fashion Fairies
- ☐ The Sugar & Spice Fairies
- ☐ The Earth Fairies
- ☐ The Magical Crafts Fairies
- ☐ The Baby Animal Rescue Fairies
- ☐ The Fairy Tale Fairies

■ SCHOLASTIC

Find all of your favorite fairy friends at
scholastic.com/rainbowmagic

HIT entertainment

RMFAIRY

RAINBOW magic™

Which Magical Fairies Have You Met?

- ❏ Joy the Summer Vacation Fairy
- ❏ Holly the Christmas Fairy
- ❏ Kylie the Carnival Fairy
- ❏ Stella the Star Fairy
- ❏ Shannon the Ocean Fairy
- ❏ Trixie the Halloween Fairy
- ❏ Gabriella the Snow Kingdom Fairy
- ❏ Juliet the Valentine Fairy
- ❏ Mia the Bridesmaid Fairy
- ❏ Flora the Dress-Up Fairy
- ❏ Paige the Christmas Play Fairy
- ❏ Emma the Easter Fairy
- ❏ Cara the Camp Fairy
- ❏ Destiny the Rock Star Fairy
- ❏ Belle the Birthday Fairy

- ❏ Olympia the Games Fairy
- ❏ Selena the Sleepover Fairy
- ❏ Cheryl the Christmas Tree Fairy
- ❏ Florence the Friendship Fairy
- ❏ Lindsay the Luck Fairy
- ❏ Brianna the Tooth Fairy
- ❏ Autumn the Falling Leaves Fairy
- ❏ Keira the Movie Star Fairy
- ❏ Addison the April Fool's Day Fairy
- ❏ Bailey the Babysitter Fairy
- ❏ Natalie the Christmas Stocking Fairy
- ❏ Lila and Myla the Twins Fairies
- ❏ Chelsea the Congratulations Fairy
- ❏ Carly the School Fairy
- ❏ Angelica the Angel Fairy
- ❏ Blossom the Flower Girl Fairy

SCHOLASTIC

Find all of your favorite fairy friends at
scholastic.com/rainbowmagic

3 stories in each one!

HIT entertainment

RMSPECIAL17

Visit Friendship Forest, where animals can talk and magic exists!

Meet best friends Jess and Lily and their adorable animal pals in this enchanting series from the creator of Rainbow Magic!

scholastic.com

MAGIC